moose
TRACKS!

To my handsome husband, Scott,
who leaves tracks on my heart as well as my floor
—K. W.

For little Nina
—J. E. D.

Margaret K. McElderry Books
An imprint of Simon & Schuster Children's Publishing Division
1230 Avenue of the Americas
New York, New York 10020

Book design by Abelardo Martínez
The text for this book is set in Fink Heavy.
The illustrations are rendered in acrylic, watercolor, and ink.

Manufactured in China
4 6 8 10 9 7 5 3

Library of Congress Cataloging-in-Publication Data
Wilson, Karma.
Moose tracks! / by Karma Wilson ; illustrated by Jack E. Davis.—1st ed.
p. cm.
Summary: A homeowner remembers visits from all the animals whose tracks, feathers,
and other traces are visible—except for the moose whose prints are everywhere.
ISBN-13: 978-0-689-83437-0
ISBN-10: 0-689-83437-3
[1. Moose—Fiction. 2. Animal tracks—Fiction. 3. Animals—Fiction.
4. Stories in rhyme.] I. Davis, Jack E., ill. II. Title.
PZ8.3.W6976 Mo 2006
[E]—dc21
00-028374

MOOSE
TRACKS!

by **Karma Wilson**

illustrated by **Jack E. Davis**

Margaret K. McElderry Books
New York London Toronto Sydney

There are moose tracks on my back porch. I'm not sure how they got there.

One thing I'm fairly certain of—
last night those tracks were NOT there.

There is bear hair on my lawn chair,
but a bear came by to eat.
When we barbecued our supper,
he shed hair there on his seat.

Bear hair, I remember.
But *who* left all these moose tracks?

There are moose tracks in my kitchen, and I'm itchin' to know why! Some friends dropped over yesterday, but not one moose stopped by.

There are nut shells on the counter,
but a chipmunk left them there.
He was making nut fudge sundaes
for the two of us to share.

Nut shells, I remember.
But *who* left all these moose tracks?

There are moose tracks on the den floor.
How they got there, I can't say.
Last night there were no moose tracks,
and they're everywhere today!

There are feathers on my carpet,
but my best pal is a goose.
We were playing hokey-pokey,
and her feathers fluttered loose.

Feathers, I remember.
But *who* left all these moose tracks?

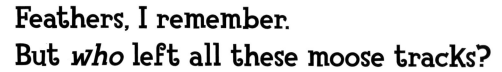

There are moose tracks in my bathroom.
It's an all-out mystery!
If I only knew who left them,
he could mop them up for me.

There are mouse prints in my bathtub,
but my maid, she is a mouse.
And she's always leaving wee prints
when she tidies up my house.

Mouse prints, I remember.
But *who* left all these moose tracks?

There are moose tracks in my bedroom.
They are spattered all around.
Noisy moose feet should have clattered,
but I never heard a sound!

There are wood chips in my guest bed,
but a beaver spent the night.
He got hungry, and the bedpost
looked so good, he took a bite.

Wood chips, I remember.
But *who* left all these moose tracks?

There are moose tracks
on my back porch,
in my kitchen and my den,

in my bathroom
and my bedroom—

moose tracks
everywhere
I've been!